A BARTIMAEUS GRAPHIC NOVEL

The Amulet of Samarkand

ADAPTED BY
JONATHAN STROUD
AND **ANDREW DONKIN**

ART BY
LEE SULLIVAN

COLOR BY
NICOLAS CHAPUIS

LETTERING BY
CHRIS DICKEY

Disney · HYPERION BOOKS
New York

Adapted from the Bartimaeus novel *The Amulet of Samarkand*

Text copyright © 2010 by Jonathan Stroud
Illustrations copyright © 2010 by Lee Sullivan

Printed in the United States of America
F322-8368-0-10213
First Edition
10 9 8 7 6 5 4 3 2 1
ISBN: 978-1-4231-1146-7 (hardcover)
Library of Congress Cataloging-in-Publication Data on file.
ISBN: 978-1-4231-1147-4 (paperback)
Library of Congress Catalog
Card Number on file.

Visit www.HyperionBooksForChildren.com

Certified Chain of Custody
SUSTAINABLE FORESTRY INITIATIVE
35% Certified Forests,
65% Certified Fiber Sourcing
www.sfiprogram.org

AS ALWAYS, OF COURSE, I TRIED TO RESIST.

I TRIED TO COUNTERACT THE PULL, BUT THE WRENCHING WORDS WERE JUST TOO STRONG. EACH SYLLABLE WAS A HARPOON SPEARING MY SUBSTANCE, DRAGGING ME OFF.

FOR THREE SHORT SECONDS, THE GENTLE GRAVITY OF THE OTHER PLACE HELPED HOLD ME BACK...THEN, ALL AT ONCE, I WAS EXPELLED OUT INTO THE WORLD...

LONDON. COLD, GRAY, AND HEAVY WITH ODORS.

OH NO.

EVENING EDITION. LATEST NEWS!

AAARKK!

AAARKK!

CHAPTER I

BARTIMAEUS

THE TEMPERATURE OF THE ROOM DROPPED FAST. ICE FORMED ON THE CURTAINS AND CANDLES.

KRRACKLE

THE ROOM FILLED WITH A YELLOW, CHOKING CLOUD OF BRIMSTONE.

INDISTINCT BLACK SHADOWS WRITHED AND ROILED INSIDE IT.

THE CLOUD FORMED TENDRILS THAT LICKED THE AIR LIKE HUNGRY TONGUES.

SCHLUURPP

SCHLUURPP

INVISIBLE FEET PATTERED ACROSS FLOORBOARDS, AND INVISIBLE MOUTHS WHISPERED WICKED THINGS FROM BEHIND THE BED AND UNDER THE DESK.

THUB

THUB THUB

FROM FAR AWAY CAME THE SOUND OF MANY VOICES SCREAMING...

AAAIIEEE!

HEY, IT WAS HIS FIRST TIME.

I WANTED TO SCARE HIM.

FZZZT

FZZZT

FZZZT

I DID, TOO.

I CHARGE YOU... TO...TO T-T-TELL ME YOUR NAME.

HE KNEW AND I KNEW THAT HE KNEW MY NAME ALREADY.

I AM BARTIMAEUS.

OTHERWISE, HOW COULD HE HAVE SUMMONED ME IN THE FIRST PLACE? YOU NEED THE RIGHT WORDS, THE RIGHT ACTIONS, AND MOST OF ALL, THE RIGHT NAME.

I SAW HIM GIVE A GULP. GOOD, HE KNEW MY REPUTATION.

ARE YOU THAT BARTIMAEUS WHO IN OLDEN TIMES WAS SUMMONED BY THE MAGICIANS TO REPAIR THE WALLS OF PRAGUE AND WHO DID—

WHAT A TIME WASTER THIS KID WAS.

I UPPED THE VOLUME A BIT ON THIS ONE.

I AM BARTIMAEUS! I AM SAKHR AL-JINNI, N'GORSO THE MIGHTY, AND SERPENT OF SILVER PLUMES! I HAVE REBUILT THE WALLS OF URUK, KARNAK, AND PRAGUE. I HAVE SPOKEN WITH SOLOMON. I HAVE WATCHED OVER OLD ZIMBABWE TILL THE STONES FELL AND THE JACKALS FED ON ITS PEOPLE.

I AM BARTIMAEUS! I RECOGNIZE NO MASTER! SO I CHARGE YOU, **BOY**. WHO ARE YOU TO SUMMON ME?

IMPRESSIVE STUFF, EH? ALL TRUE AS WELL, WHICH GAVE IT EVEN MORE POWER.

I RATHER HOPED HE WOULD BE BLUSTERED INTO TELLING ME HIS NAME OR STEPPING OUTSIDE THE CIRCLE SO I COULD NAB HIM.

NO LUCK THERE, THEN.

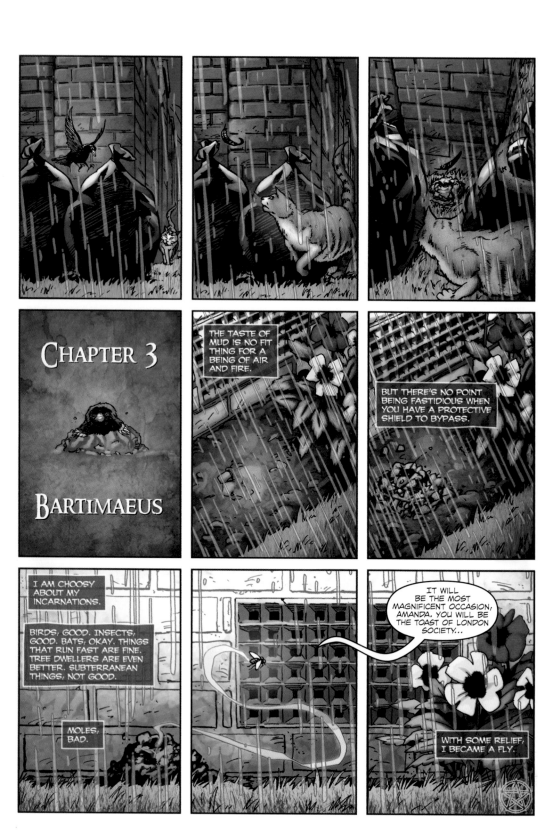

CHAPTER 3

BARTIMAEUS

THE TASTE OF MUD IS NO FIT THING FOR A BEING OF AIR AND FIRE.

BUT THERE'S NO POINT BEING FASTIDIOUS WHEN YOU HAVE A PROTECTIVE SHIELD TO BYPASS.

I AM CHOOSY ABOUT MY INCARNATIONS.

BIRDS, GOOD. INSECTS, GOOD. BATS, OKAY. THINGS THAT RUN FAST ARE FINE. TREE DWELLERS ARE EVEN BETTER. SUBTERRANEAN THINGS, NOT GOOD.

MOLES, BAD.

IT WILL BE THE MOST MAGNIFICENT OCCASION, AMANDA. YOU WILL BE THE TOAST OF LONDON SOCIETY...

WITH SOME RELIEF, I BECAME A FLY.

TWO HUMANS WERE SITTING UNDERNEATH A HIDEOUS CRYSTAL THING THAT WAS PRETENDING TO BE A CHANDELIER.

AND YOU'RE SURE THE PRIME MINISTER WILL COME?

AMANDA, HE IS VERY MUCH LOOKING FORWARD TO VIEWING YOUR ESTATE.

I MEMORIZED THE WOMAN INSTANTLY. I WOULD APPEAR IN HER GUISE TOMORROW WHEN I WENT BACK TO VISIT THAT KID. ONLY NAKED. LET'S SEE HOW HIS ADOLESCENT MIND COPED WITH THAT.

CHAPTER 4

BARTIMAEUS

ON THE SECOND PLANE, I SAW AN IMP FLOATING OVER LOVELACE'S SHOULDER ON THE LOOKOUT FOR DANGER.

EVEN WITH YOUR MANY RIVALS HOUNDING HIM THESE LAST FEW WEEKS?

DESPITE THEIR CONSTANT EFFORTS TO HAVE IT MOVED, HE HAS REMAINED COMMITTED TO HOLDING THE CONFERENCE AT YOUR DELIGHTFUL HALL.

YOU'VE ALWAYS KNOWN HOW TO PLAY THE P.M., SIMON. HOW TO FLATTER HIS VANITY.

IT WAS A PITY I WASN'T A SPIDER. THEY CAN SIT FOR HOURS.

FLIES ARE MORE JITTERY, AND I HAD TO FORCE MY UNWILLING BODY TO LURK.

KEEP IT TO YOURSELF, MY LOVE, BUT ALL HE REALLY HAS LEFT NOW IS CHARM, AND MOST DAYS HE DOESN'T EVEN BOTHER WITH THAT.

PARDON ME SIR, BUT THE CARS ARE READY.

IT PAINS ME, AMANDA, BUT DUTY CALLS. I MUST RETURN TO PARLIAMENT.

MY GOOD FRIEND MAKEPEACE HAS SENT THE TICKETS FOR HIS PLAY, SO I SHALL SEE YOU AT THE THEATER TOMORROW EVENING.

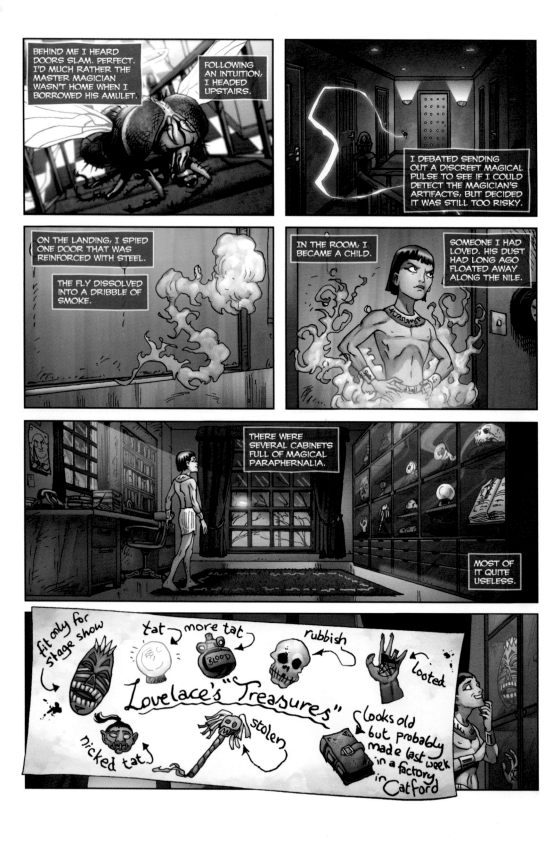

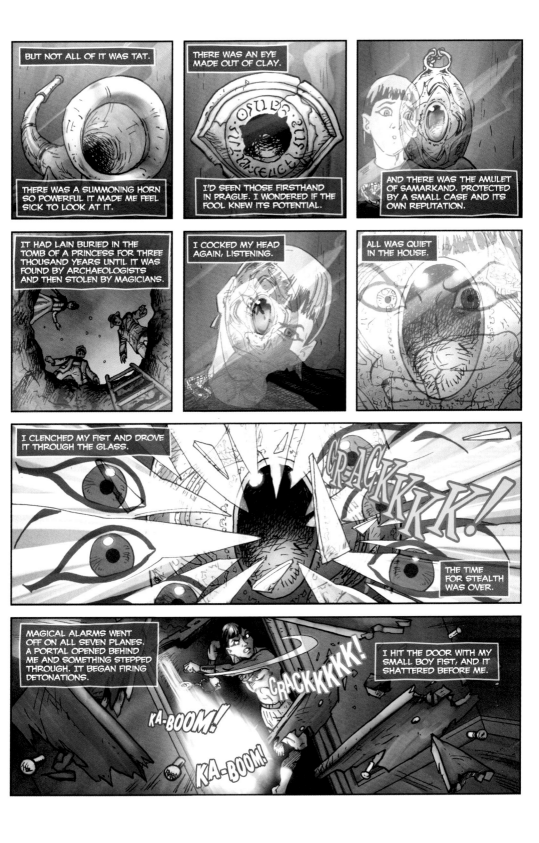

FOOM!

FOOM!

I HAD TO GET OUT OF THE HOUSE, AND FAST.

I RAN THROUGH SEVERAL ROOMS, EACH TIME MAKING A BREAK FOR THE WINDOW...

...AND EACH TIME RETREATING WHEN ONE OR MORE OF THE SENTRIES APPEARED.

KA-BOOM!

KA-BOOM!

I FOUND MYSELF IN THE KITCHEN, AND WITH GROWING FRUSTRATION SAW THE THREE SENTINELS APPEAR AGAIN. I PUT A SEAL ON THE DOOR TO STOP WHATEVER WAS CHASING ME AND TO BUY SOME TIME.

HELLO... BARTIMAEUS.

STILL RUNNING AWAY FROM JABOR, EH?

I FELT A SLIGHT UNEASE.

I CHECKED OUT THE COOK. ON PLANES ONE TO SIX HE WAS THE SAME, BUT ON THE SEVENTH PLANE...UH-OH...TENTACLES.

HELLO, FAQUARL.

HOW'S IT GOING?

NOT BAD.

HAVEN'T SEEN YOU AROUND.

NO, GUESS NOT.

HIGHGATE,
NORTH LONDON.

BEFORE.

"Above all, there is one fact that we must drive into your wretched little skull now so that you never forget it."

"Yes, sir."

"Do you know what that fact is?"

"No, sir."

"No? Well then, boy, I shall tell you. It is this. Demons are very, very wicked. They will hurt you if they can. Do you understand?"

"Yes, sir."

I cannot stop watching his eyebrows.

ARE YOU SURE, BOY?

YES, SIR. I UNDERSTAND. DEMONS ARE VERY, VERY WICKED AND WILL HURT YOU IF THEY CAN.

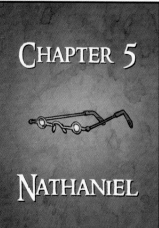

CHAPTER 5

NATHANIEL

WELL NOW, YOU SAY YES, AND I AM SURE YOU MEAN YES — AND YET...

I DO NOT FEEL CONVINCED THAT YOU REALLY, TRULY UNDERSTAND.

"Go to my study, boy. On my desk is a box. In the box is a pair of spectacles. Put them on and come back to me. Simple, yes?"

I had never been allowed in this room before.

STOP! B-...
BEGONE!

Then I remembered the spectacles.

Chapter 6

Bartimaeus

I FLEW FROM HAMPSTEAD AT TOP SPEED AND TOOK SHELTER UNDER THE EAVES OF A DESERTED HOUSE BY THE THAMES.

I PREENED MY FEATHERS AND WATCHED THE SKY.

AS I EXPECTED, THE MAGICIAN SENT OUT SEARCH SPHERES TO HUNT DOWN HIS AMULET.

ONE OF THE PROBLEMS WITH POWERFUL MAGICAL ARTIFACTS IS THAT THEY HAVE A DISTINCTIVE PULSATING AURA THAT'S ABOUT AS SUBTLE AS A NAKED MAN AT A FUNERAL.

I KNEW I HAD TO KEEP MOVING.

SO I CONTINUED MY FRANTIC, FUGITIVE DANCE ACROSS LONDON. THE URCHIN HAD FORBIDDEN ME TO RETURN BEFORE DAWN AND I WOULD BE EXHAUSTED LONG BEFORE THAT.

LONDON

TOUR LONDON

I DECIDED ON A NEW PLAN. I WOULD DROWN OUT THE AMULET'S PULSE BY MINGLING WITH THE GREAT UNWASHED — IN OTHER WORDS, WITH PEOPLE.

I WAS THAT DESPERATE.

FISH & CHIPS

MAGICAL CHARMS

TOURS

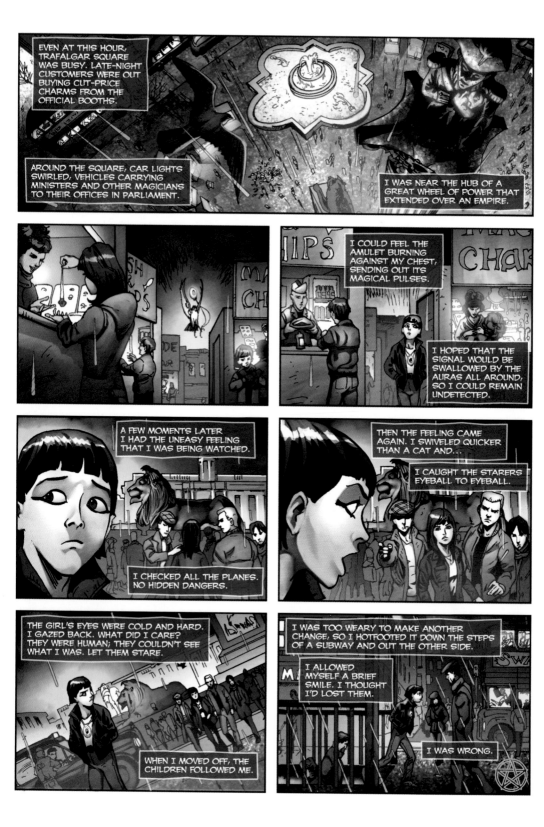

CHAPTER 7

BARTIMAEUS

THE OLD PAIN HAD STARTED UP AGAIN, THROBBING IN MY STOMACH AND THROUGH MY BONES. IT WASN'T HEALTHY TO BE ENCASED IN A PHYSICAL BODY FOR SO LONG.

THE AMULET BEAT AGAINST MY CHEST WITH EVERY STEP. I WOULD HAVE HAPPILY LOBBED IT INTO THE NEAREST TRASH CAN, BUT I WAS BOUND BY MY ORDERS FROM THAT KID.

THE MASSED DARKNESS OF THE HIGH BUILDINGS CLOSED IN ON EITHER SIDE, OPPRESSING ME.

CITIES GET ME DOWN, ALMOST AS IF I WERE UNDERGROUND.

THEY MAKE ME LONG FOR THE SOUTH.

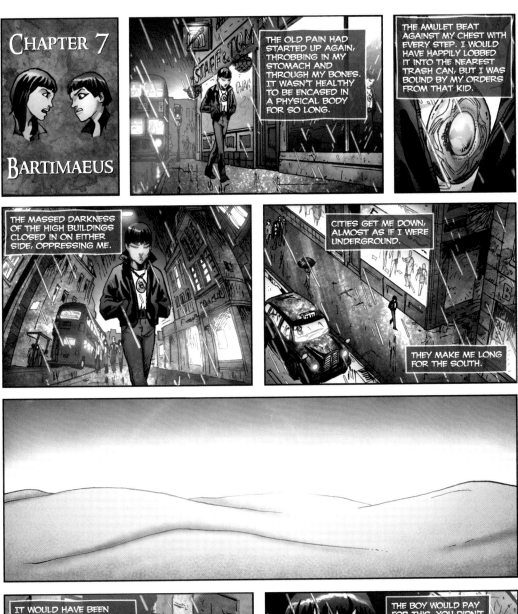

IT WOULD HAVE BEEN A LOT MORE AGREEABLE TO RETURN TO THE URCHIN IMMEDIATELY TO RID MYSELF OF THE AMULET.

BUT MAGICIANS ALMOST ALWAYS INSIST ON SUMMONING US AT SPECIFIC TIMES. IT REMOVES THE POSSIBILITY OF OUR CATCHING THEM AT A (POTENTIALLY FATAL) DISADVANTAGE.

THE BOY WOULD PAY FOR THIS. YOU DIDN'T REDUCE BARTIMAEUS OF URUK TO DOSSING IN DOORWAYS AND GET AWAY WITH IT.

THEN I HEARD SOMETHING. FOOTSTEPS IN THE ALLEY.

THE UNDERWOOD HOUSE, HIGHGATE.

BEFORE.

I REALLY DO NOT SEE WHY WE HAVE TO HAVE THE CHILD ACTUALLY LIVING IN THE HOUSE, MARTHA.

YOU MIGHT ENJOY IT, DEAR.

I AM NOT GOING TO ENJOY IT.

AND THESE EGGS ARE TOO RUNNY AGAIN.

SORRY, DEAR.

CHAPTER 8

NATHANIEL

I HAVE NEVER HAD AN APPRENTICE AND I DO NOT WANT ONE.

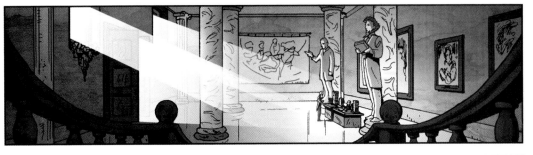

I'M UNDERWOOD, YOUR MASTER. YOUR TRUE LIFE BEGINS NOW. COME WITH ME.

I MADE A BIG SHOW OF CHECKING THE LINES OF THE CIRCLE.

AHA! YOU'VE SPELLED THIS WRONG! AND YOU KNOW WHAT THAT MEANS!

THE KID'S FACE WENT AN INTERESTING MIX OF WHITE AND RED AS HE STUDIED THE LINES HIMSELF.

RECREANT DEMON! THE PENTACLE IS SOUND – IT BINDS YOU STILL!

OKAY, I LIED. NOW DO YOU WANT THIS OR NOT?

I WATCHED HIM CLOSELY. IF ONE FOOT OR ONE FINGER FELL OUTSIDE THE CIRCLE, I WOULD BE ON HIM FASTER THAN A PRAYING MANTIS. SADLY, HE PRODUCED A STICK.

EUCH, THIS IS DISGUSTING!

BLAME ROTHERHITHE SEWAGE WORKS AND THE DEMONIC HORDES OF LONDON THAT WERE CHASING ME.

YOU WERE PURSUED?

YOU SOUND ALMOST PLEASED. WRONG EMOTION, KID. TRY FEAR.

WELL, NO MATTER. I HAVE CARRIED OUT MY CHARGE. MY TASK IS DONE. FOR THE REMAINDER OF YOUR SHORT LIFE, FAREWELL!

YOU CANNOT DEPART! I HAVE OTHER WORK FOR THEE. ADELBRAND'S PENTACLE HOLDS YOU AT MY COMMAND.

MORE THAN THE RENEWED CAPTIVITY, IT WAS THE OCCASIONAL ARCHAISMS THAT ANNOYED ME SO MUCH. I ASK YOU... "THEE" AND "RECREANT DEMON"?!

BARTIMAEUS, I CHARGE YOU TO TAKE THE AMULET OF SAMARKAND AND HIDE IT IN THE MAGICAL REPOSITORY OF THE MAGICIAN ARTHUR UNDERWOOD, CONCEALING IT SO THAT HE CANNOT OBSERVE IT.

THEN YOU ARE TO RETURN TO ME IMMEDIATELY TO AWAIT FURTHER INSTRUCTIONS.

VERY WELL. WHERE DOES THIS UNFORTUNATE MAGICIAN RESIDE?

DOWNSTAIRS.

OUCH.

I WAS HEADING UP TO THE ATTIC ROOM AGAIN... WHEN THINGS GOT RATHER INTERESTING.

THE BOY WAS HEADING DOWNSTAIRS, TRAILING IN THE WAKE OF THE MAGICIAN'S WIFE.

HE LOOKED THOROUGHLY FED UP.

THIS WAS BAD. HE HAD LOST CONTROL OF THE SITUATION, A DANGEROUS THING FOR ANY MAGICIAN.

HE'S IN THERE. GO STRAIGHT IN...

...NATHANIEL.

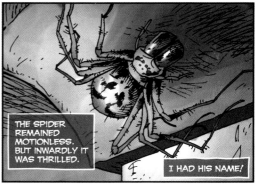

THE SPIDER REMAINED MOTIONLESS. BUT INWARDLY IT WAS THRILLED.

I HAD HIS NAME!

WHAT ARE THE SIX WORDS OF DIRECTION? ANY LANGUAGE.

APPARE; MANE; AUSCULTA; SE DEDE; PARE; REDI: APPEAR; REMAIN; LISTEN; SUBMIT; OBEY; RETURN.

BE FAIR, SIMON. HE CAN'T KNOW THAT YET!

BRAVO.

STANDARDS MUST HAVE DROPPED IF A BACKWARD APPRENTICE CAN BE CONGRATULATED FOR SPOUTING SOMETHING WE ALL LEARNED AT OUR MOTHERS' TEATS.

YOU'RE...

...YOU'RE JUST A SORE LOSER.

YOU COCKSURE GUTTERSNIPE. YOU'RE HELPLESS. YOU KNOW A FEW WORDS, BUT YOU'RE CAPABLE OF NOTHING.

GET OUT OF MY SIGHT.

LEAVE US, BOY.

"You're helpless."

"You're capable of nothing."

"You're helpless."

"You're capable of nothing."

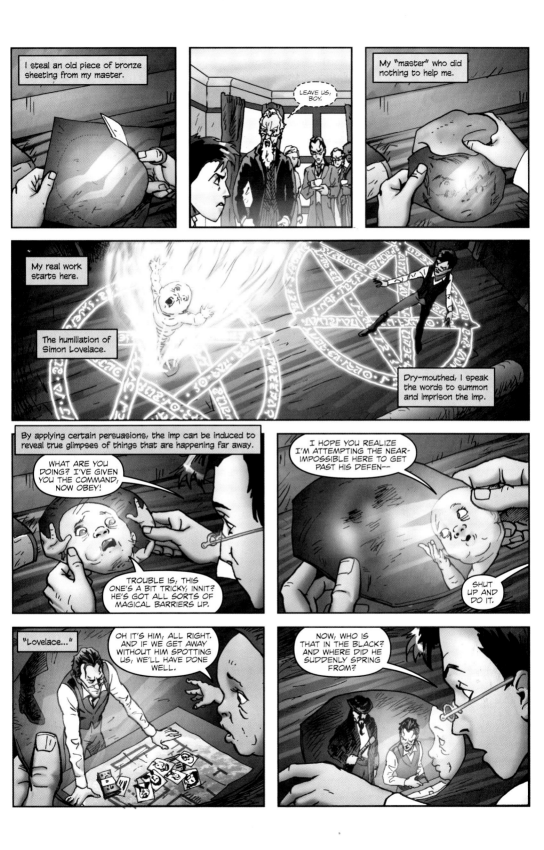

NOW.

I KNEW IT WAS GOING TO BE A DECENT SCRAP, AND I FIGURED WHAT WOULD ANNOY HIM MOST WAS TO APPEAR AS ANOTHER BOY OF ABOUT THE SAME AGE.

HE CAME OUT FIGHTING THOUGH, I'LL GIVE HIM THAT.

I CHARGE YOU TO--

NATHANIEL, EH? VERY POSH. DOESN'T REALLY SUIT YOU.

THAT'S NOT MY TRUE NAME.

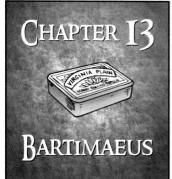

CHAPTER 13

VIRGINIA PLAIN

BARTIMAEUS

AS I HOPED, HE FORGOT HIMSELF AND WENT FOR THE OBVIOUS ATTACK.

NATHANIEL.

AND USING HIS BIRTH NAME I SENT IT STRAIGHT BACK AT HIM.

ZZZZKKKK-KKKKK

CAREFUL.

NEARLY TOOK YOUR OWN HEAD OFF.

I KNOW A WAY YOU'LL STILL OBEY ME.

THE MOMENT YOU'VE GONE ON YOUR NEXT TASK, I SHALL CAST A SPELL OF INDEFINITE CONFINEMENT, BINDING YOU INTO THIS TIN.

UNFORTUNATELY FOR ME, HE WAS AN UNUSUALLY CLEVER AND RESOURCEFUL CHILD.

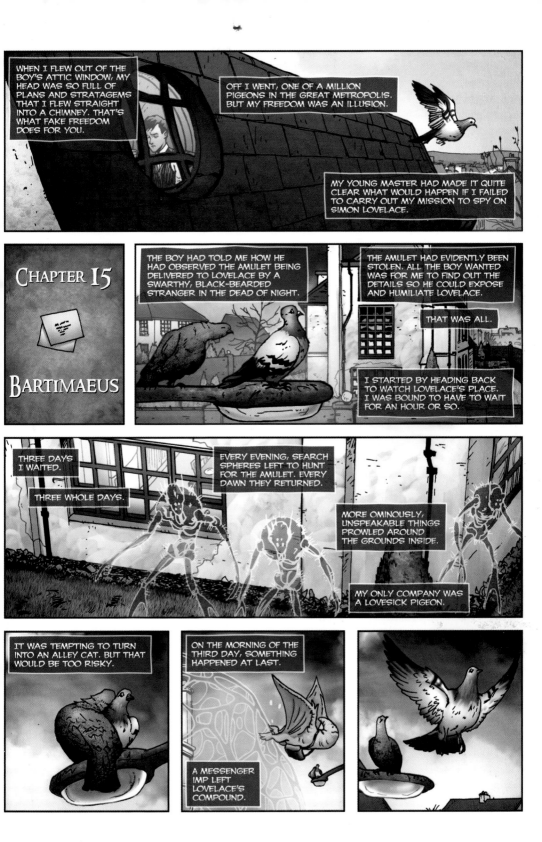

SOME SOCIETIES I HAD KNOWN MADE GREAT USE OF MESSENGER IMPS.

THE ROOFTOPS AND DATE PALMS OF OLD BAGHDAD USED TO SWARM WITH THE THINGS AFTER BREAKFAST AND SHORTLY BEFORE SUNDOWN.

I FOLLOWED AT A DISCREET DISTANCE AND WHEN WE WERE IN A REMOTE AREA I CHANGED AGAIN...

AND SWOOPED DOWN ON THE UNLUCKY IMP.

WHACKKKKK!

YOU CAN STICK YOUR QUESTIONS UP YOUR--

FIRST, I'M GOING TO READ THE LETTERS YOU'RE CARRYING. THEN I'M GOING TO ASK YOU SOME QUESTIONS ABOUT SIMON LOVELACE. OKAY?

THIS REPLACES A SHORT, CENSORED EPISODE CHARACTERIZED BY BAD LANGUAGE AND SOME SADLY NECESSARY VIOLENCE. WHEN WE PICK UP THE STORY AGAIN EVERYTHING IS AS BEFORE, EXCEPT THAT I AM PERSPIRING SLIGHTLY AND THE CONTRITE IMP IS THE MODEL OF COOPERATION.

HERE ARE THE LETTERS, O MOST BOUNTEOUS AND MERCIFUL ONE. ONE IS TO RUPERT DEVEREAUX, THE PRIME MINISTER.

THE OTHER I AM UNDER ORDERS TO DELIVER TO THE RESIDENCE OF MR. SCHYLER IN GREENWICH.

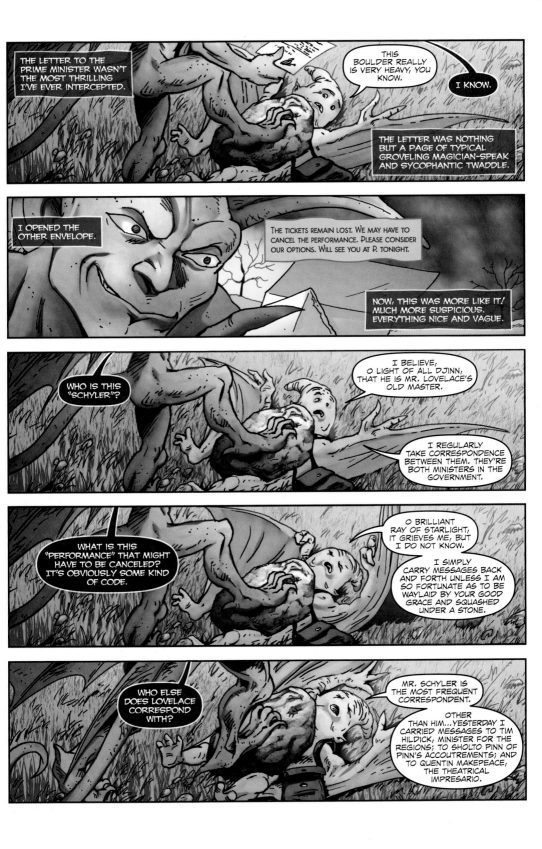

PINN'S ACCOUTREMENTS LOOKED LIKE A PALACE THAT HAD BEEN DROPPED ONTO THE STREET BY A GANG OF KNACKERED DJINN.

I GOT THERE JUST IN TIME TO SEE AN IMMENSELY FAT MAN PUT A "CLOSED" SIGN ON THE DOOR AND HAIL A CAB.

I TOOK THIS TO BE SHOLTO PINN HIMSELF.

CHAPTER 16

BARTIMAEUS

I KNOCKED ANYWAY. LOUDLY. THE BOY WHO ANSWERED...

MESSAGE HERE FOR MR. SHOLTO FROM SIMON LOVELACE.

HE'S OUT. COME BACK LATER.

...WAS REALLY A FOLIOT ON THE SECOND PLANE.

DON'T WORRY, I'LL WAIT.

I'M NOT SUPPOSED TO LET ANYONE IN...HEY.

WOW. NOT MANY PEOPLE GET TO WORK IN A PLACE THIS POSH.

YOU'RE CERTAINLY RIGHT THERE.

STILL, I BET YOU PROBABLY GET STUCK WITH ALL THE HEAVY LIFTING AND CLEANING, EH?

YOU CHEEKY FUNGUS! THE MASTER VALUES ME MORE THAN THAT. I AM HIS ASSISTANT!

I KNEW THEN THAT I WAS DEALING WITH A COLLABORATOR OF THE WORST KIND.

I ENGAGED HIM WITH SICKENING FLATTERY FOR SEVERAL MINUTES BEFORE GETTING DOWN TO BUSINESS.

YOU HAD ANYTHING FAMOUS IN HERE, THEN?

THE HIGHLIGHT OF LAST YEAR WAS NEFERTITI'S ANKLE BRACELET. THAT WAS A SENSATION!

ALL A BIT OVER MY HEAD, GUV'NOR. I'LL TELL YOU SOMETHING I'VE HEARD OF...THAT AMULET OF SAMARAD THING?

YOU MEAN THE AMULET OF SAMARKAND, AND THERE YOU SHOW YOUR IGNORANCE.

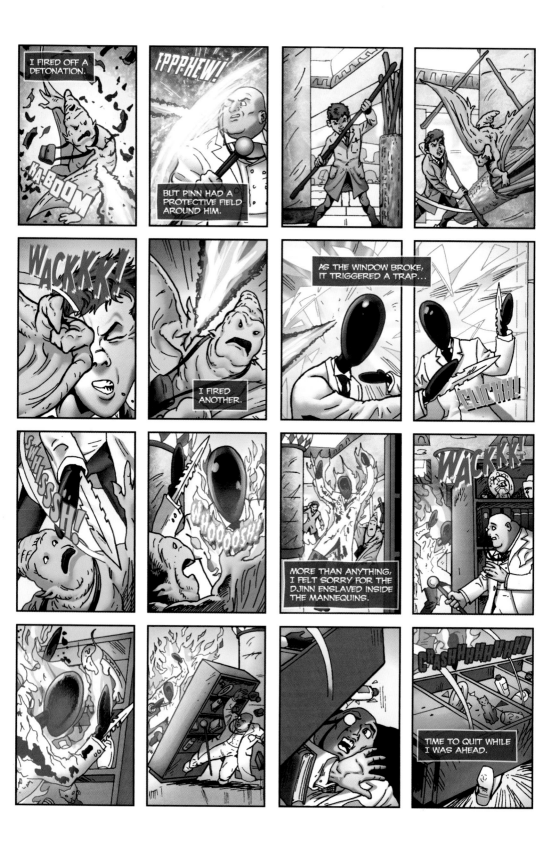

YOU'VE HURT THE MASTER.

ANYWAY, IT'S TOO LATE FOR YOU. I'VE SOUNDED THE ALARM. THE AUTHORITIES HAVE SENT AN AF--

YEAH, YEAH.

I CHANGED INTO A FALCON. HE WASN'T EXPECTING THAT, BUT WHAT DID HE KNOW?

I SHOT OVER HIS HEAD, LEAVING A LITTLE FAREWELL DROPPING TO REMEMBER ME BY.

I BURST OUT AT LAST INTO THE FREEDOM OF THE AIR.

UPON WHICH, A NET OF SILVER THREADS DRAGGED ME DOWN TO THE COLD PAVEMENT.

THE THREADS HUNG TO ME WITH THE AGONIZING TOUCH OF SILVER.

I COULD NOT CHANGE.

I COULD NOT WORK ANY MAGIC, GREAT OR SMALL.

SOMEWHERE, I HEARD SIMPKIN LAUGHING, LONG AND SHRILL.

MY MIND WAS POISONED. DARKNESS SWATHED THE FALCON AND, AS IF IT WERE A GUTTERING CANDLE, SNUFFED ITS INTELLIGENCE OUT.

CHAPTER 18

NATHANIEL

I DO LOVE TO WATCH THE FAMOUS ONES... SUCH A PLEASURE.

"That's Mr. Duvall, the Chief of Police. I met him once, John—what a charming man."

SHOULDN'T WE... YOU KNOW... TALK TO SOMEONE?

I THOUGHT I TOLD YOU TO KEEP QUIET, BOY.

"That's Maurice Schyler. He's something in the Government. I don't know what."

OH, AND THAT'S QUENTIN MAKEPEACE, THE PRIME MINISTER'S FAVORITE PLAYWRIGHT.

"Don't tell Mr. Underwood, but I think he's rather marvelous. His plays are so romantic."

"Jessica Whitwell, she's something to do with Security. Caught those Czech infiltrators ten years ago."

"Good heavens!"

"That's the merchant, Sholto Pinn.

"Whatever happened to him? Poor soul."

I feel suddenly reduced to insignificance.
The unrated apprentice of an unrated magician.

AND OF COURSE YOU KNOW *HIM*...FROM THAT RATHER UNFORTUNATE INCIDENT LAST YEAR.

"That's the Junior Minister for Trade—Simon Lovelace."

CHAPTER 19
NATHANIEL

The sphere shatters and the elementals trapped inside recoil from each other with ferocious and savage force.

Air, earth, fire, and water.

People are blown backwards.

Pelted with rocks.

Lacerated with fire.

And deluged with water.

The crowd is sent sprawling like skittles.

Night Police swarm over the river terrace.

The Prime Minister has already gone, whisked away to safety by a powerful afrit.

Most of the crowd weren't so lucky.

I find Mrs. Underwood and feel a little teary with relief.

ARE YOU ALL RIGHT?

YES. I THINK SO. BUT WHERE'S ARTHUR?

I spot him looking rather dazed.

ANYONE SEE WHAT HAPPENED?

AN ENORMOUS BLACK RAVEN SWOOPED DOWN, FOLLOWED BY ANOTHER ONE.

THERE WAS A BLUR OF MOVEMENT, A SNAP, AND TWO GULPS.

THEN THE TWO UTUKKU WERE GONE.

EVEN I DON'T SEE *THAT* EVERY DAY.

ONE OF THE RAVENS GAVE A SHIMMY AND TOOK ON AN ALL-TOO-FAMILIAR GUISE...

OH. HELLO.

HELLO, BARTIMAEUS.

CHAPTER 24

BARTIMAEUS

AND JABOR, TOO. HOW NICE OF YOU BOTH TO COME.

WE THOUGHT YOU MIGHT BE LONELY, BARTIMAEUS.

NOW, TELL US WHERE YOU SECRETED THE AMULET OF SAMARKAND AND IF YOU SPEAK RAPIDLY, WE MIGHT HAVE TIME TO DESTROY THE ORB BEFORE YOU PERISH.

REVERSE THAT SEQUENCE AND YOU COULD HAVE YOURSELVES A DEAL.

WE BOTH KNOW THAT IF I TELL YOU THE LOCATION, YOU'LL LEAVE ME TO DIE. THEREFORE, I'LL OBVIOUSLY GIVE YOU FALSE INFORMATION JUST TO SPITE YOU. SO ANYTHING I SAY FROM IN HERE WILL BE WORTHLESS. AND THAT MEANS YOU'VE GOT TO LET ME OUT.

ANNOYING, BUT I SEE YOUR POINT.

THE KINDLY MAGICIANS WHO PUT ME IN HERE MENTIONED LEGIONS OF HORLAS AND UTUKKU—I SHOULD THINK THAT'S THEM ARRIVING NOW... I DOUBT EVEN JABOR CAN SWALLOW THEM ALL.

SO PERHAPS WE COULD CONTINUE THIS DISCUSSION A LITTLE LATER?

AGREED.

PALE-FACED HORLAS FOUGHT TO GET OUT OF THE PORTAL, HOLDING THEIR LITTLE TRIDENTS AND SILVER NETS IN THEIR STICK-THIN ARMS.

IT WAS TIME TO GO.

CCCCKKKKKKKKKKKKKKKKKKK!

FROM A POCKET IN HIS COAT, FAQUARL PRODUCED A RING OF IRON SOLDERED TO A METAL ROD. (WELL, HE WOULDN'T WANT TO TOUCH THE IRON—UGH!)

Fiiizzzzzzzz

MARVELOUS. IF ONLY WE'D HAD A DRUM ROLL.

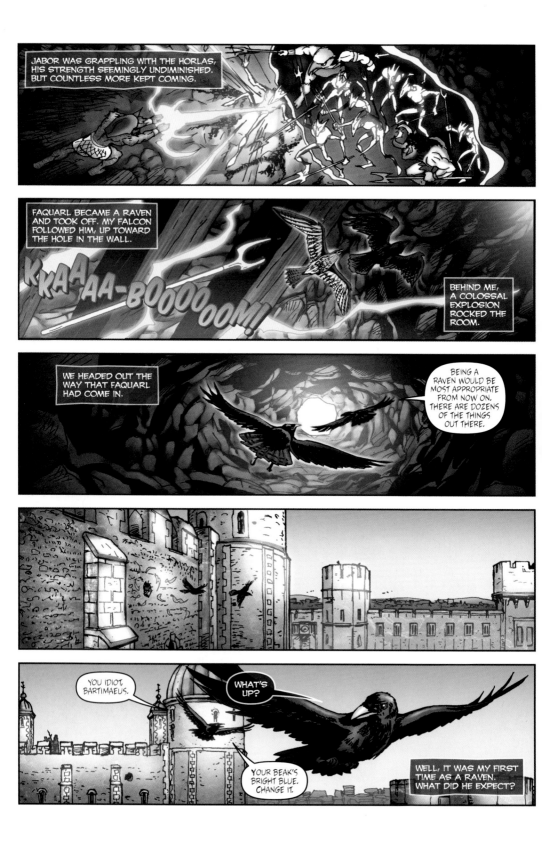

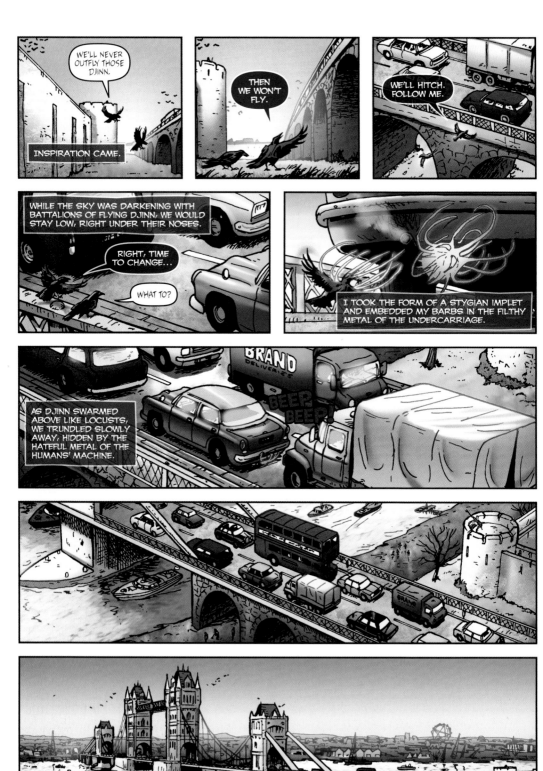

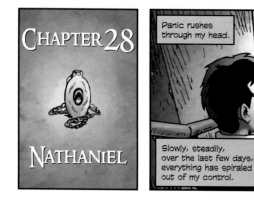

Chapter 28

Nathaniel

Panic rushes through my head.

Slowly, steadily, over the last few days, everything has spiraled out of my control.

I hear Mrs. Underwood gently humming as she hurries around downstairs.

Mrs. Underwood... who I have placed in terrible danger.

Running and hiding are the advice of a treacherous demon. Not the actions of an honorable magician.

I know what I must do.

I arrive just in time to witness the moment of discovery.

HA! WELL, WELL, WHAT HAVE WE HERE?

NO... IT'S A TRICK... YOU'RE FRAMING ME. I DON'T KNOW HOW THAT GOT THERE...

HE'S TELLING THE TRUTH. *I* TOOK IT.

THE PERSON THAT YOU WANT IS ME.

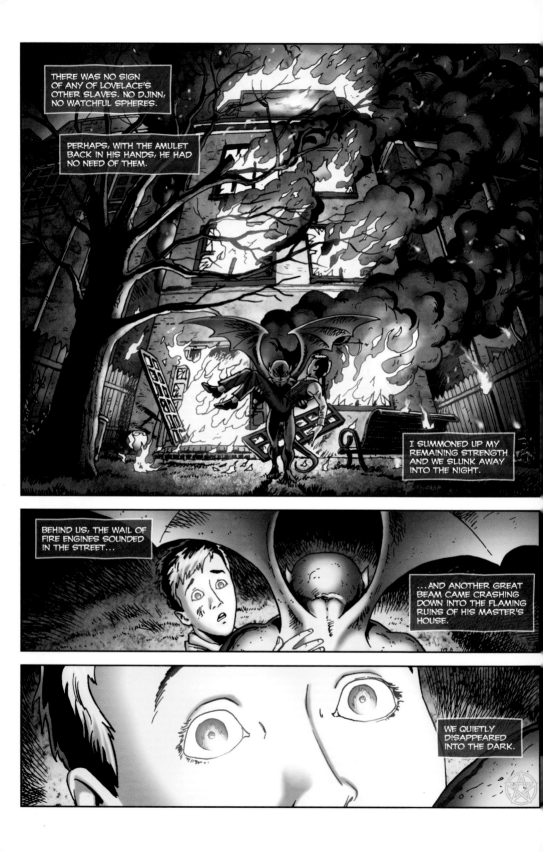

OR, OF COURSE, YOU COULD JUST READ THIS...

Conference of the Year

DEVEREAUX

CATHCART

HEDDLEHAM HALL

LOVELACE

"Bartimaeus, fly to Heddleham Hall now, get as close as you can, and find us a way to get in. Then return to me.

"I shall wait for you here. I need to sleep.

"Now go."

CHAPTER 32

NATHANIEL

HA HA HA

Fury overcomes dizziness and I set off in unsteady pursuit.

UHHHHHH

I strain to hear their words and edge nearer.

CLINK!

WHAAGGGKK!

SHALL I CUT HIS THROAT FOR YOU, KITTY?

NO... HE'S ONLY A STUPID KID. LET'S GO.

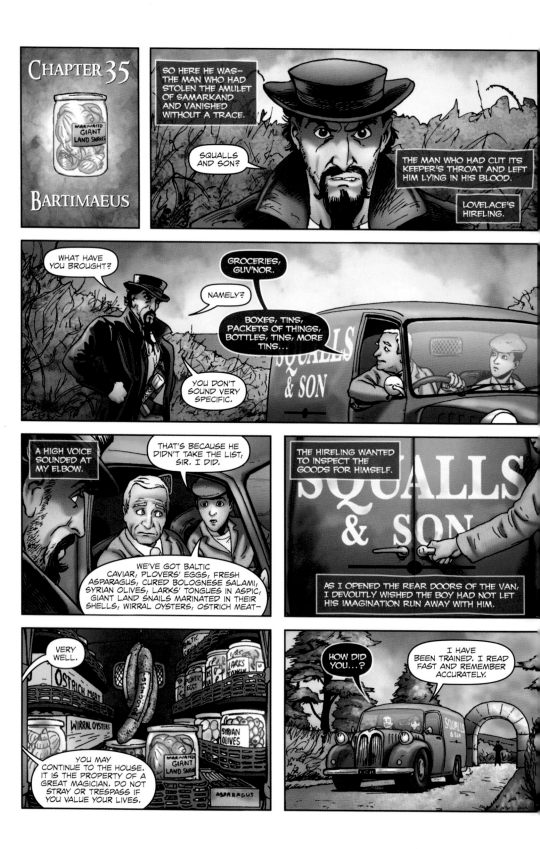

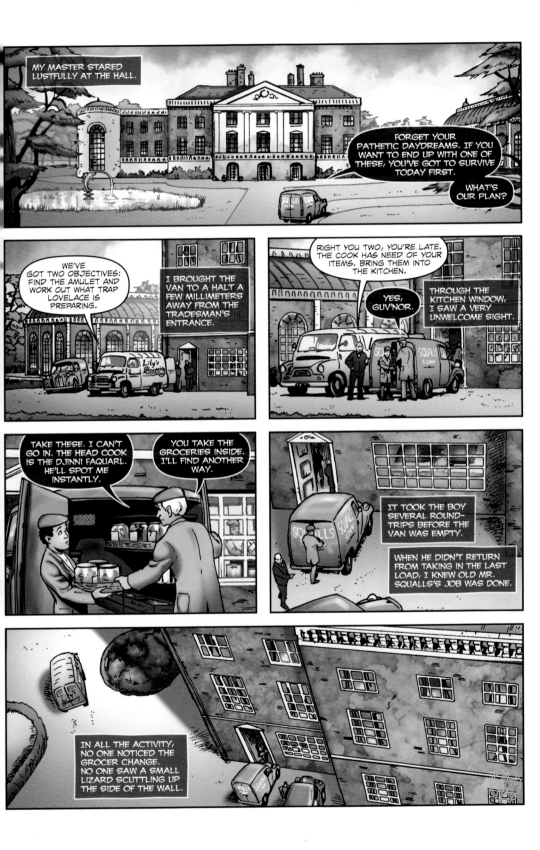

I could be caught at any moment, but I feel a strange exhilaration.

I'm taking control of events.

I'm the one doing the hunting.

CHAPTER 36

NATHANIEL

I follow a boy about my size to the cloakroom.

WHACK!

I leave him gagged and bound and hidden in a cubicle.

LIKE ANIMALS, AREN'T THEY? BLOODY MAGICIANS.

I watch Lovelace smiling at his guests. Mrs. Underwood died because he stole the Amulet. Now I will destroy him.

I SAW THE ROOM FOR THE FIRST TIME ONLY THIS MORNING. SIMON SAID IT WOULD TAKE MY BREATH AWAY. AND HE WAS RIGHT.

THE CARPET HAS TO BE SEEN TO BE BELIEVED!

THANK GOODNESS--FOOD! FAMISHING JOURNEY FROM LONDON.

ARE YOU SERVING THOSE, BOY, OR TAKING THEM FOR A WALK?

SORRY, SIR.

CHAPTER 42

BARTIMAEUS

TYPICAL OF THE KID, THAT WAS.

CHAPTER 43

BARTIMAEUS

SUNSET. THE DAY AFTER THE GREAT SUMMONING.

I PREFERRED YOUR OLD PLACE. THIS ONE SMELLS AND YOU HAVEN'T EVEN MOVED IN YET.

IT DOESN'T SMELL.

THE BOY HAD SPENT ALL DAY WITH MINISTERS AND POLICE, SPINNING AN OUTRAGEOUS YARN ABOUT HOW HE AND HIS POOR DEAD MASTER HAD FOUGHT AGAINST LOVELACE'S EVIL SCHEME.

IT DOES SMELL... OF FRESH PAINT AND PLASTIC AND ALL THINGS NEW. QUITE APPROPRIATE FOR YOU... MR. MANDRAKE.

HE DIDN'T ANSWER. HE WAS BOUNDING OUT TO LOOK AT THE VIEW.

THEY'RE A LOT NEARER FROM HERE.

YES. YOUR MRS. UNDERWOOD WOULD BE PLEASED.

WE FINALLY HAD AN HOUR TO OURSELVES. I INTENDED TO MAKE IT COUNT.

MY NEW MASTER SAYS I HAVE A GREAT CAREER AHEAD OF ME.

AH YES, JESSICA WHITWELL, THE RAKE-THIN MINISTER FOR SECURITY.

I WANT TO WORK AT THE MINISTRY HUNTING THE RESISTANCE. FIRST I'LL CATCH FRED AND STANLEY...AND THAT GIRL. THEN I'LL MAKE THEM TALK...

THE PRIME MINISTER HIMSELF SAID I WAS A HERO.

YEAH? LISTEN. THAT'S THE SOUND OF PEOPLE NOT CHEERING.

THEY HAD TO KEEP IT QUIET FOR SECURITY REASONS.

THEY HAD TO KEEP IT QUIET OR THEY'D LOOK INCREDIBLY STUPID. "TWELVE-YEAR-OLD SAVES GOVERNMENT!" THEY'D HAVE BEEN LAUGHED OFF THE STREETS.

"It's not the commoners that we have to fear. It's the conspirators who got away. Lovelace and Schyler are dead, but we know Lime, the fish-faced one, escaped. And there was at least one more..."

LISTEN, YOU'VE HAD YOUR REVENGE ON LOVELACE. PERHAPS THAT TAKES AWAY A LITTLE OF YOUR PAIN— I HOPE SO.

BUT WE HAD A DEAL. I HELPED YOU, AND I SAVED YOUR LIFE SEVERAL TIMES OVER. NOW IT'S TIME TO HONOR YOUR PROMISE TO LET ME GO...